Dear Parent:

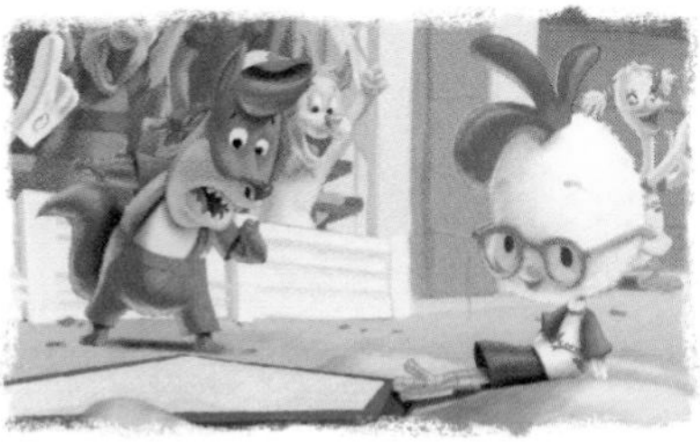

Congratulations! Your child is taking the first steps on an exciting journey. The destination? Independent reading!

STEP INTO READING® will help your child get there. The program offers five steps to reading success. Each step includes fun stories and colorful art. There are also Step into Reading Sticker Books, Step into Reading Math Readers, Step into Reading Write-In Readers, Step into Reading Phonics Readers, and Step into Reading Phonics First Steps! Boxed Sets—a complete literacy program with something for every child.

Learning to Read, Step by Step!

STEP 1
Ready to Read **Preschool–Kindergarten**
• big type and easy words • rhyme and rhythm • picture clues
For children who know the alphabet and are eager to begin reading.

STEP 2
Reading with Help **Preschool–Grade 1**
• basic vocabulary • short sentences • simple stories
For children who recognize familiar words and sound out new words with help.

STEP 3
Reading on Your Own **Grades 1–3**
• engaging characters • easy-to-follow plots • popular topics
For children who are ready to read on their own.

STEP 4
Reading Paragraphs **Grades 2–3**
• challenging vocabulary • short paragraphs • exciting stories
For newly independent readers who read simple sentences with confidence.

STEP 5
Ready for Chapters **Grades 2–4**
• chapters • longer paragraphs • full-color art
For children who want to take the plunge into chapter books but still like colorful pictures.

STEP INTO READING® is designed to give every child a successful reading experience. The grade levels are only guides. Children can progress through the steps at their own speed, developing confidence in their reading, no matter what their grade.

Remember, a lifetime love of reading starts with a single step!

For Ramona

www.stepintoreading.com

www.randomhouse.com/kids/disney

Educators and librarians, for a variety of teaching tools, visit us at www.randomhouse.com/teachers

Library of Congress Cataloging-in-Publication Data
Jordan, Apple.
The sky is falling! / by Apple Jordan ; illustrated by the Disney Storybook Artists.
    p. cm. — (Step into reading. Step 2 book)
Summary: Chicken Little is the laughingstock of the town of Oakey Oaks, but when there is an alien invasion, he saves the world and becomes a hero.
ISBN 0-7364-2318-4 (pbk) ISBN 0-7364-8042-0 (lib. bdg.)
[1. Heroes—Fiction. 2. Extraterrestrial beings—Fiction. 3. Chickens—Fiction.] I. Disney Storybook Artists. II. Title. III. Series.
PZ7.J755Sk 2005   [E]—dc22 2004029275

Printed in the United States of America   10 9 8 7 6 5 4 3 2 1

STEP INTO READING® STEP 2

Disney's
chicken little

The Sky Is Falling!

by Apple Jordan

Illustrated by the Disney Storybook Artists

Designed by Disney Publishing's Global Design Group

Random House New York

Chicken Little
made a big mistake.
He rang the town bell
to warn everyone
that the sky
was falling.

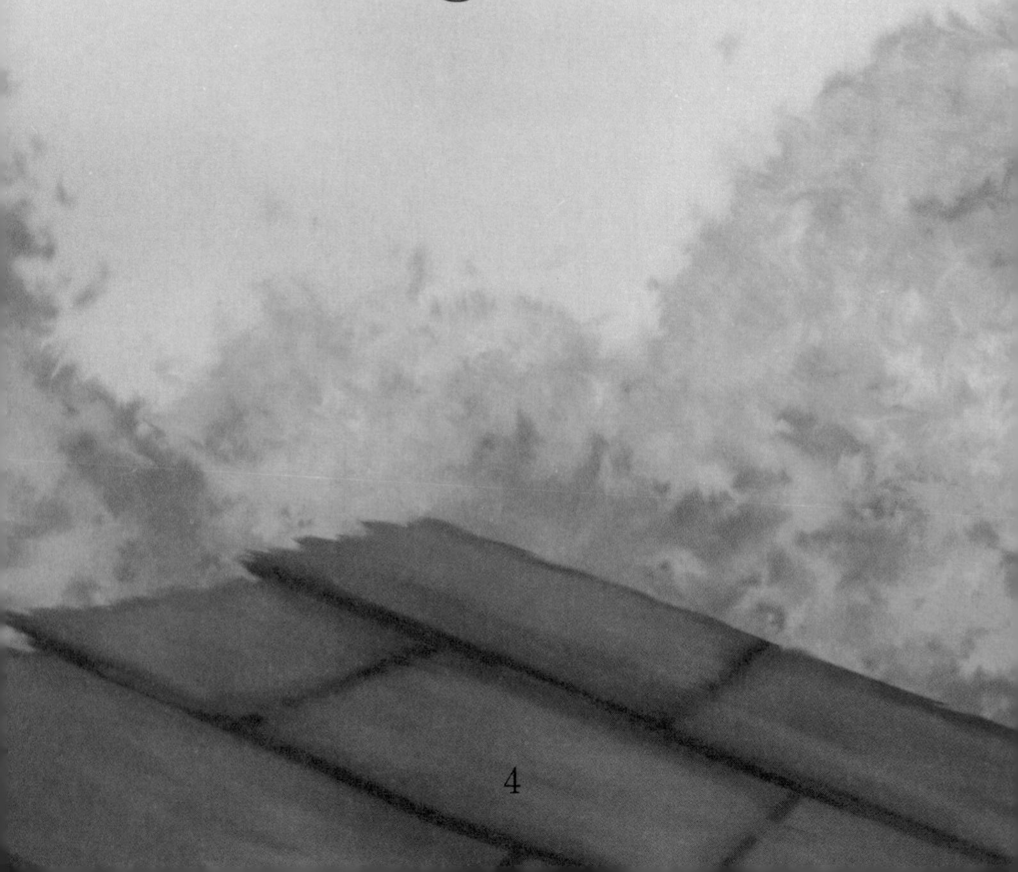

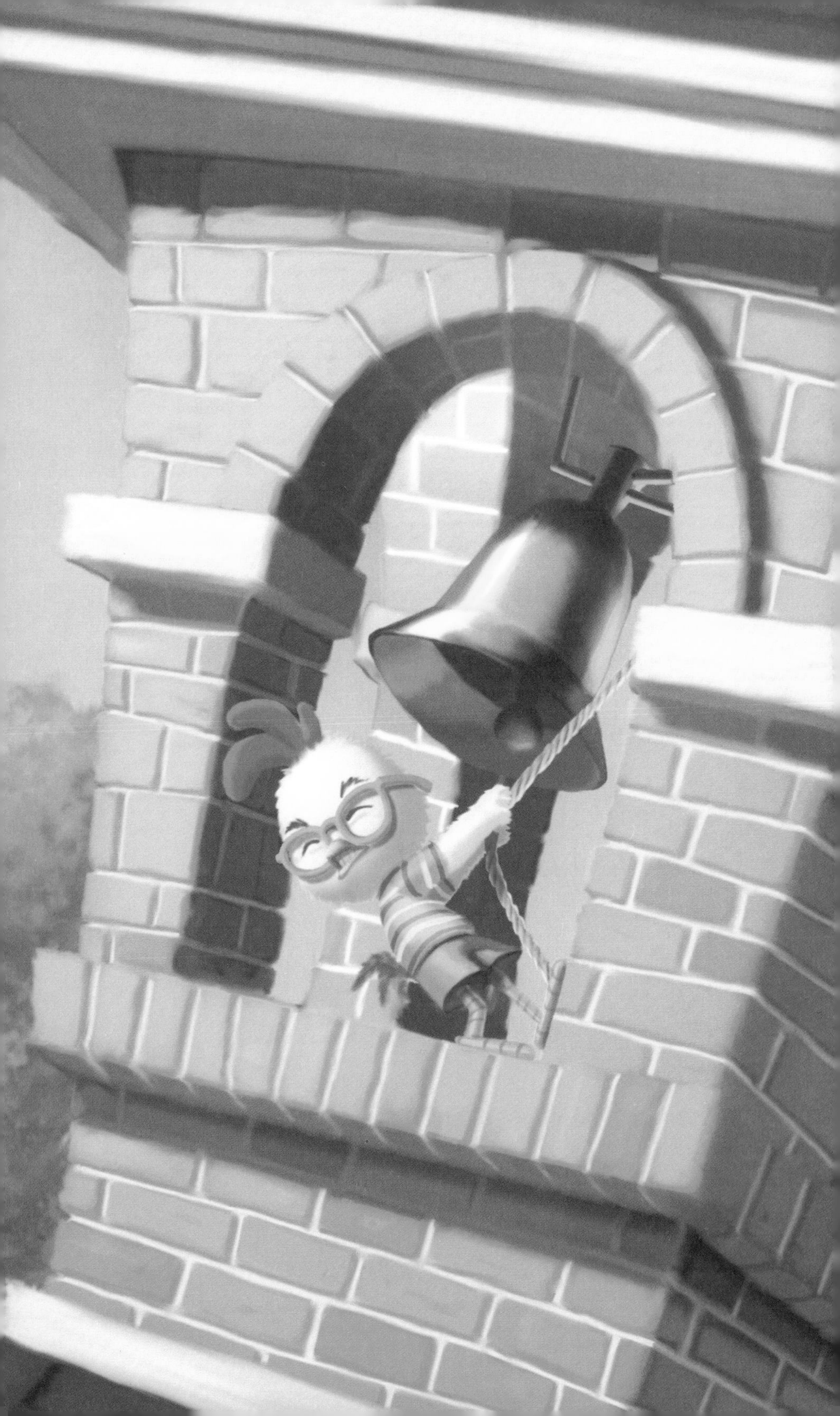

But the sky never fell.
His dad, Buck, said
it was only an acorn.

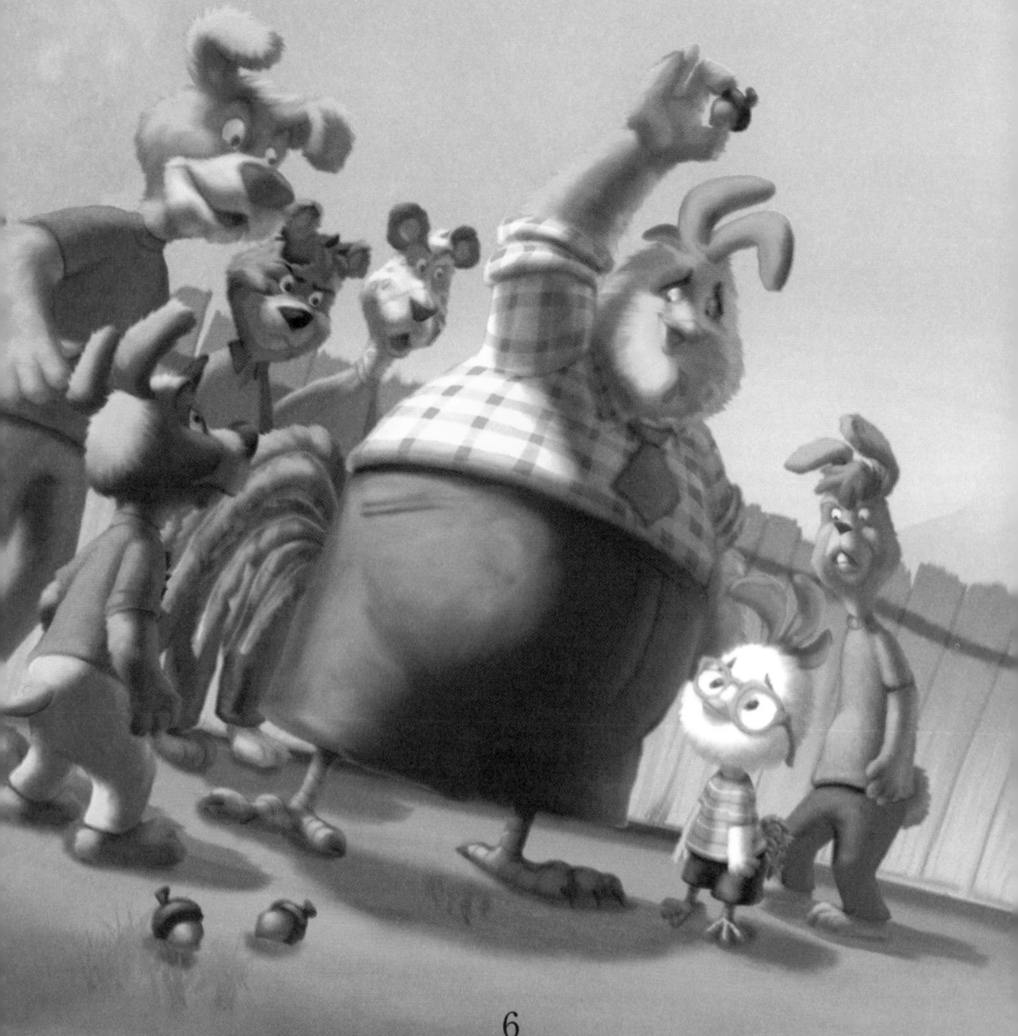

Everyone teased
Chicken Little.
No one would let him
forget his mistake.

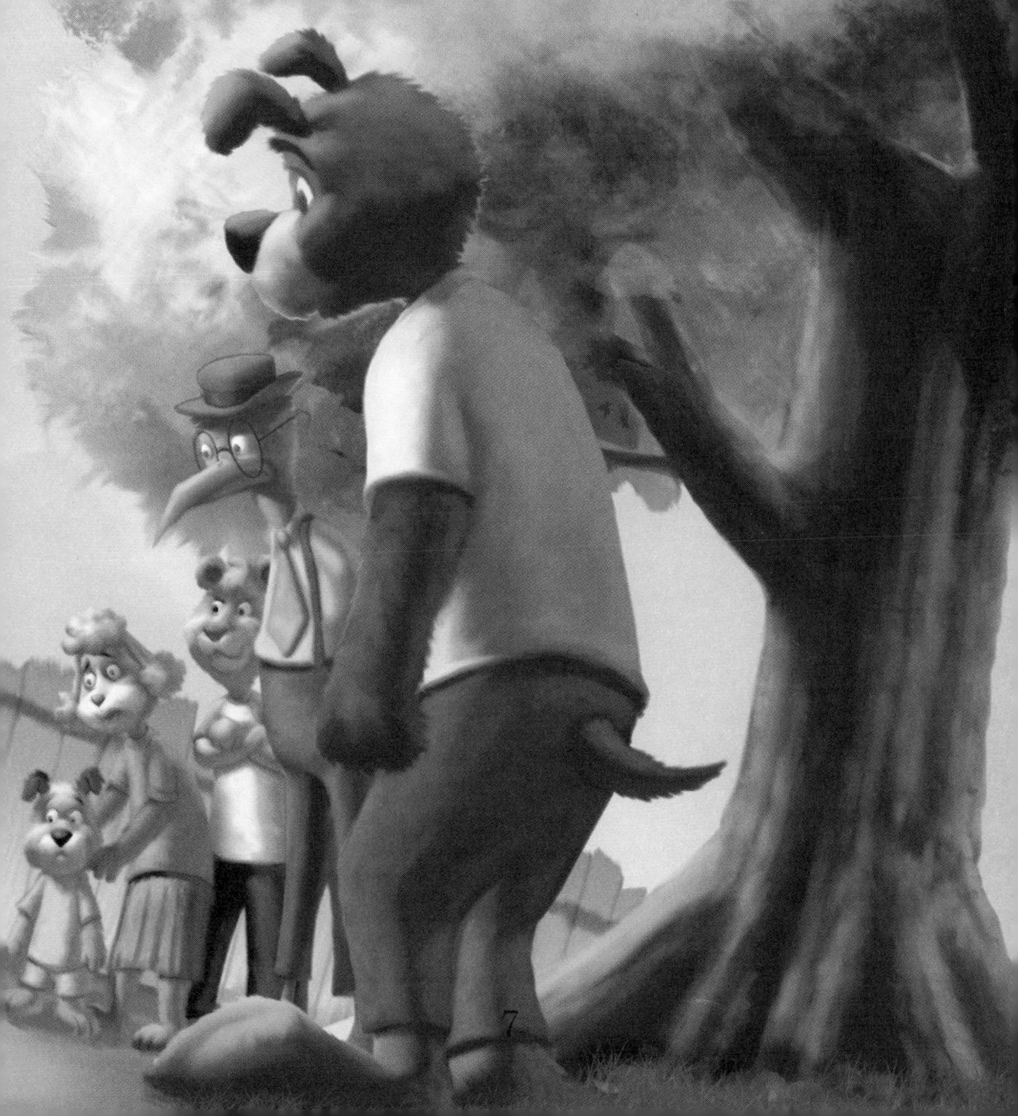

Chicken Little was tired of being teased.
He wanted things to change.
"Today is a new day," he said.

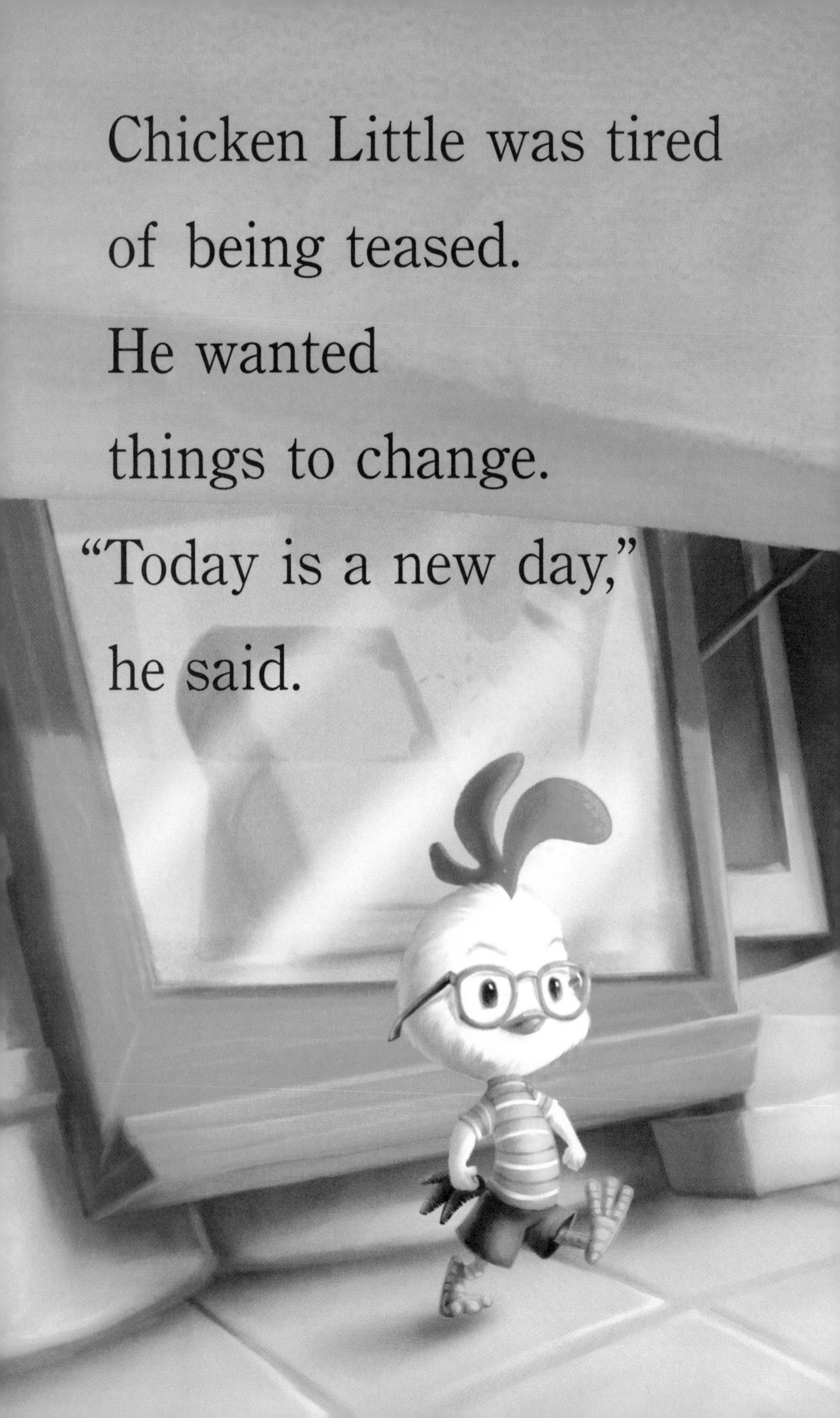

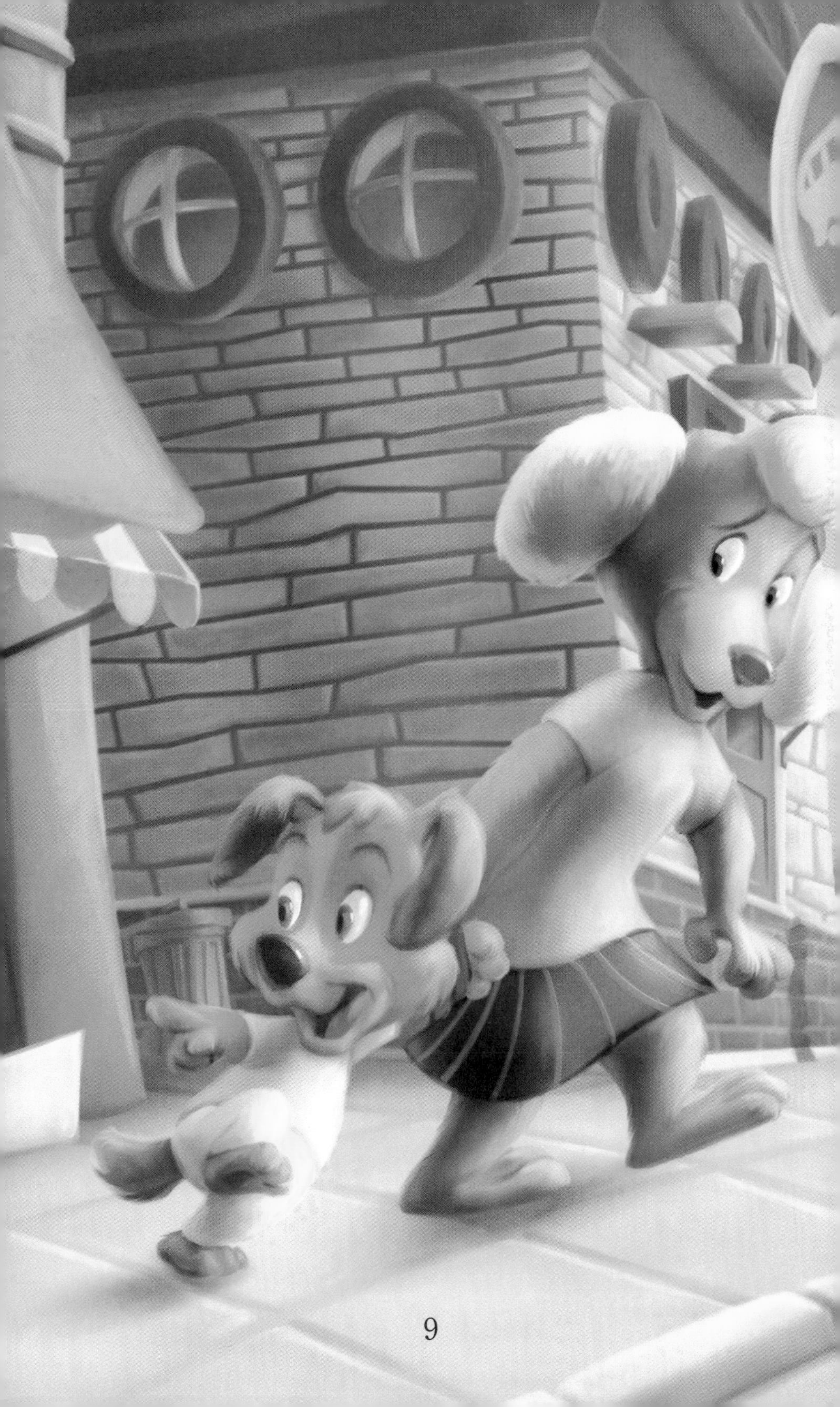

Chicken Little joined
the baseball team.
"Maybe my luck
will change,"
he thought.

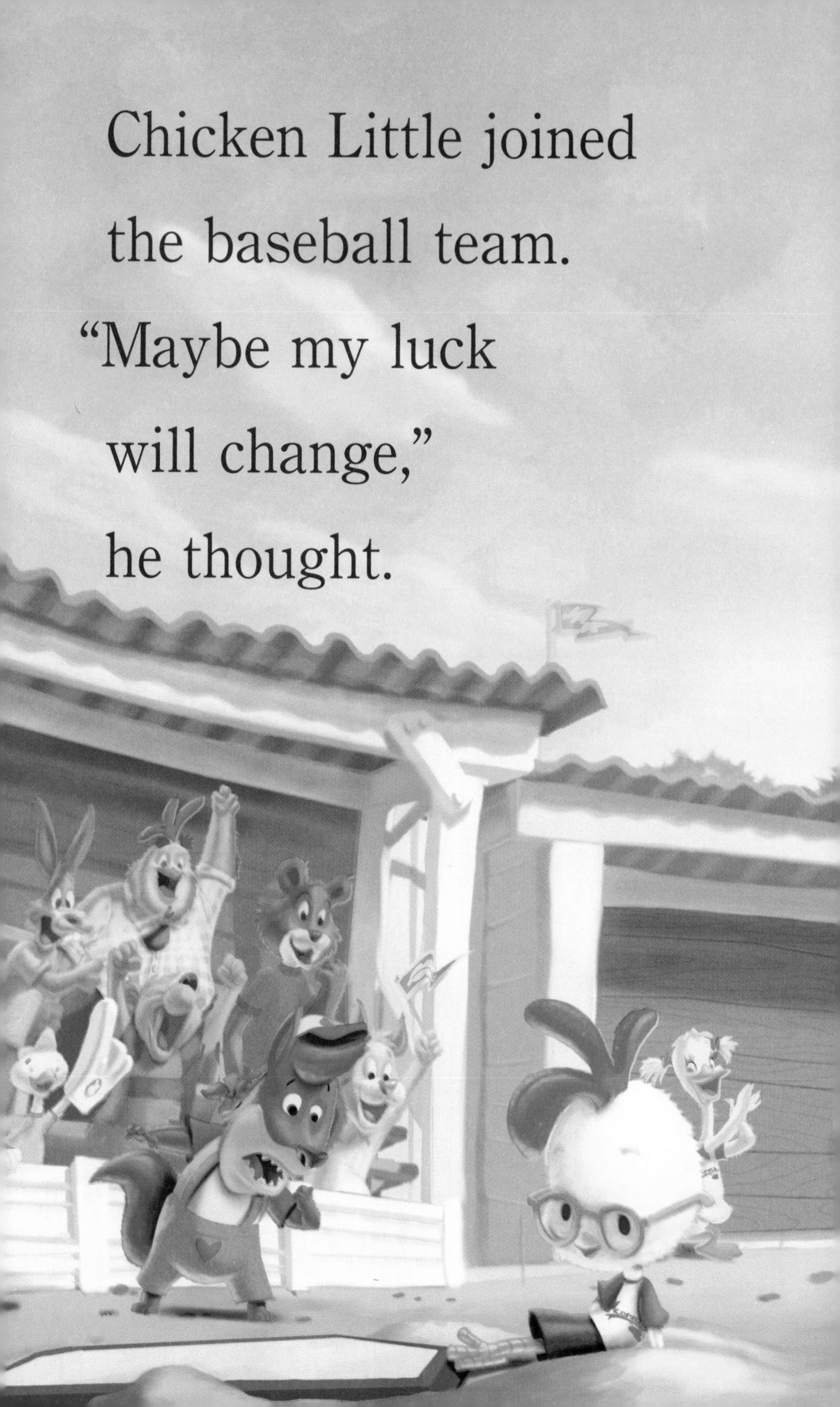

His luck did change!
He hit a home run.
He won the big game!

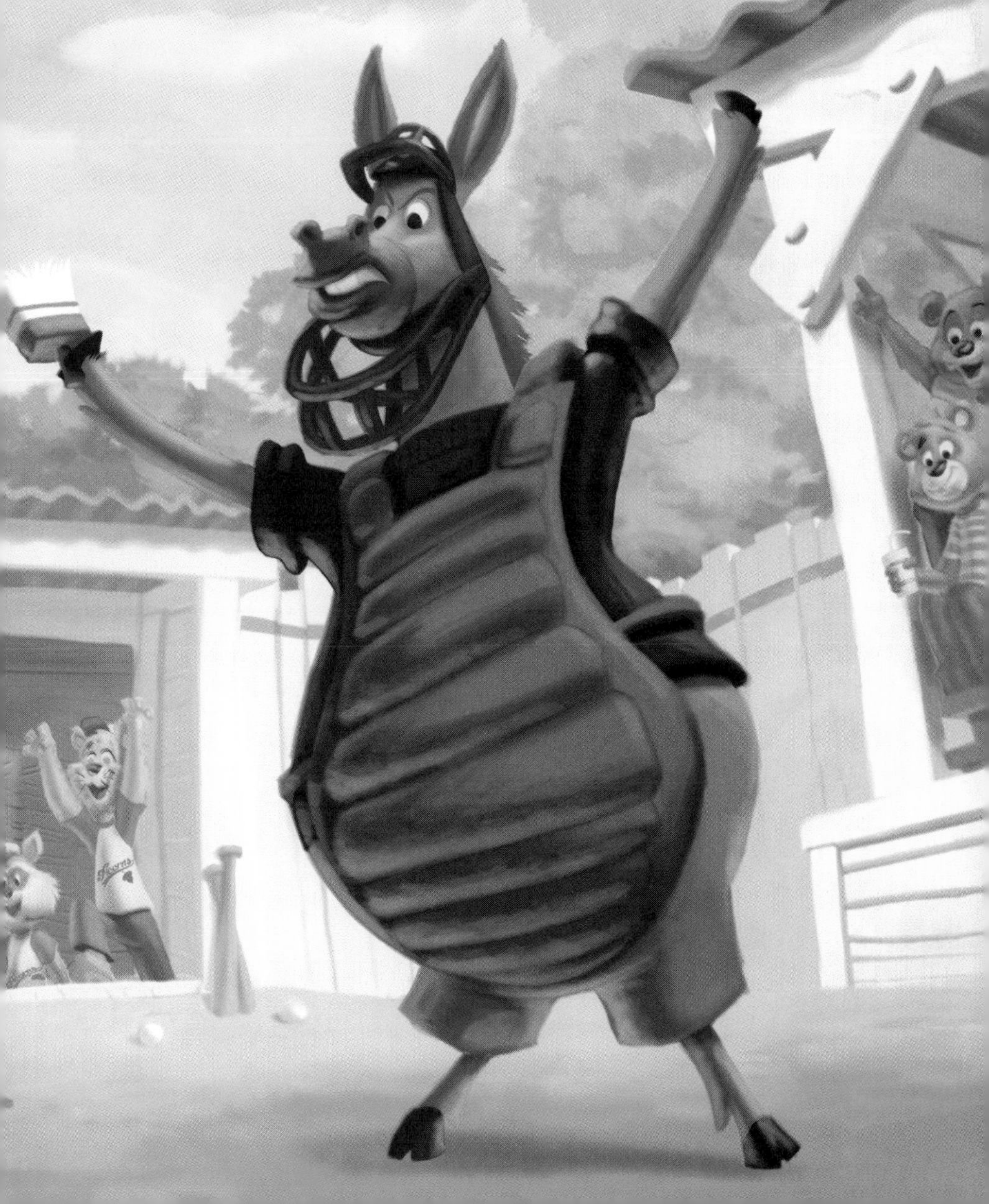

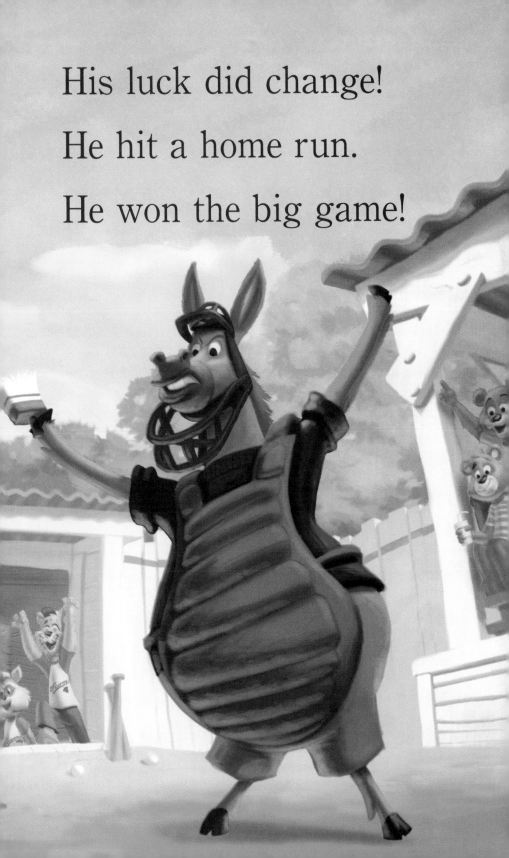

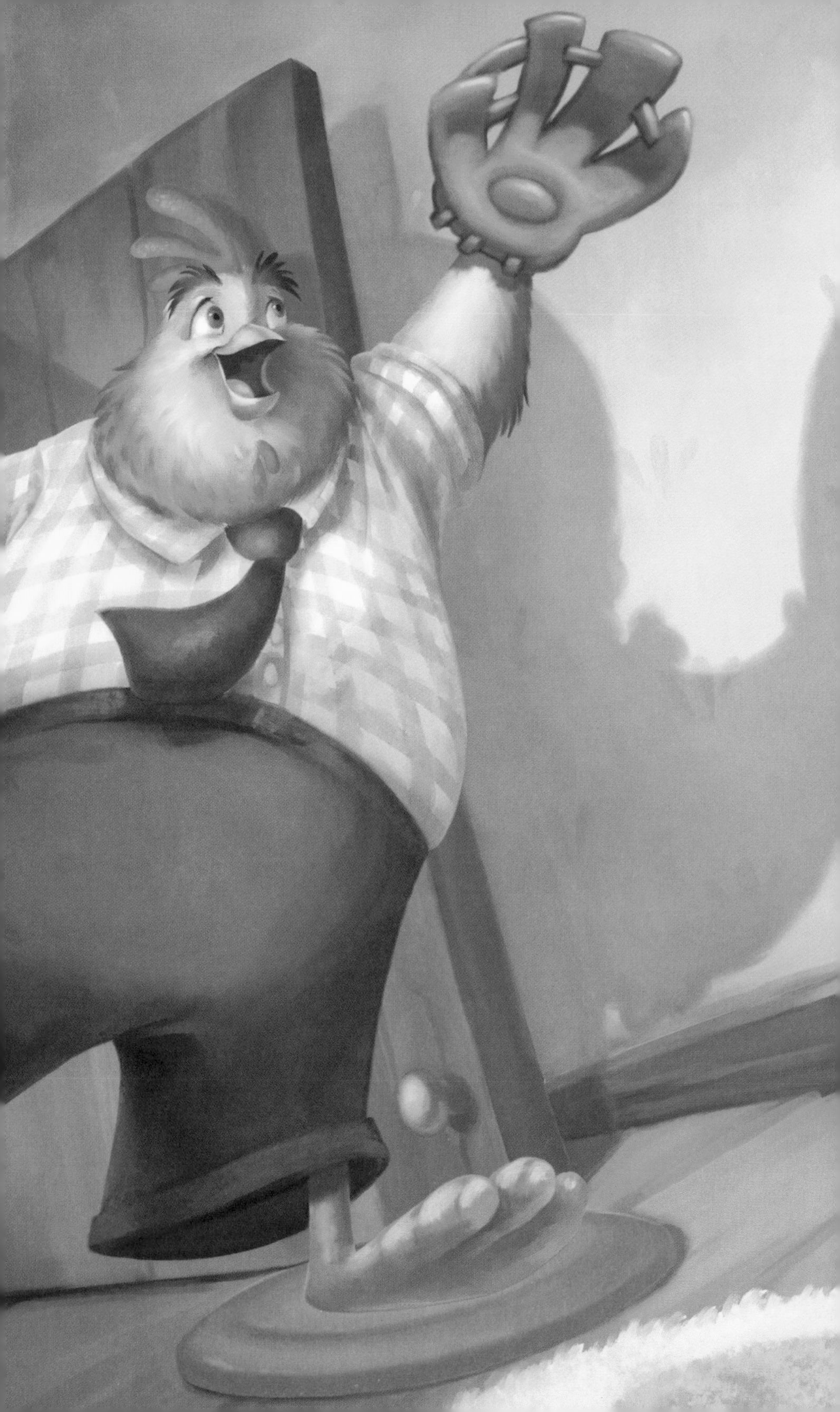

Chicken Little
was happy.
His dad was proud.
Things were better.

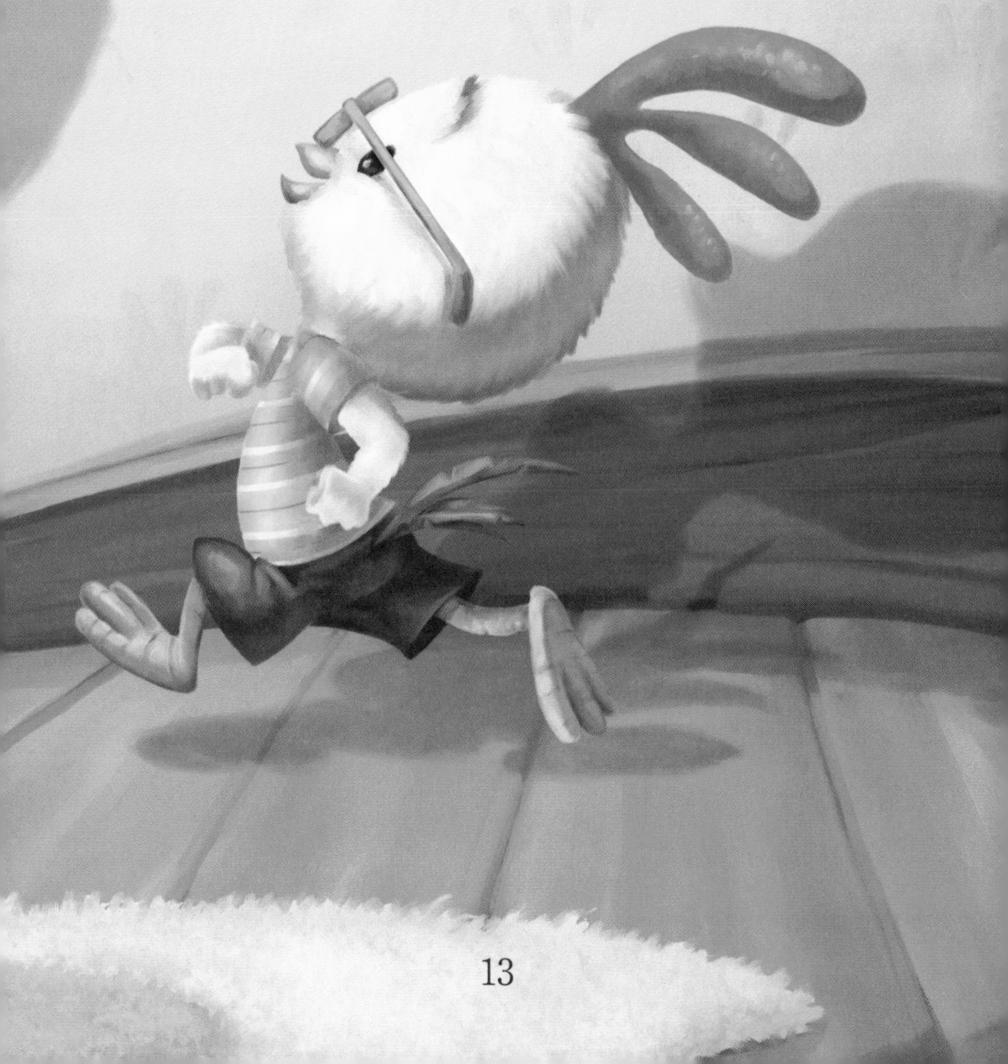

But then
there was trouble.
The sky really did fall
on Chicken Little!
A piece landed
right in his bedroom.

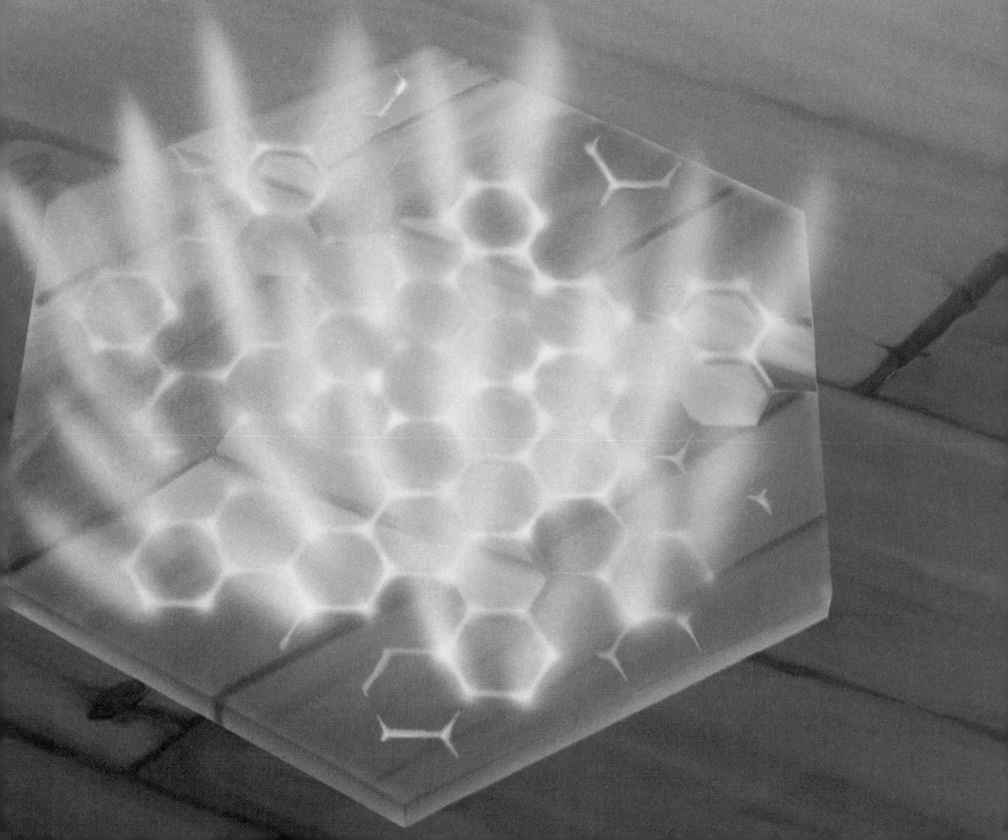

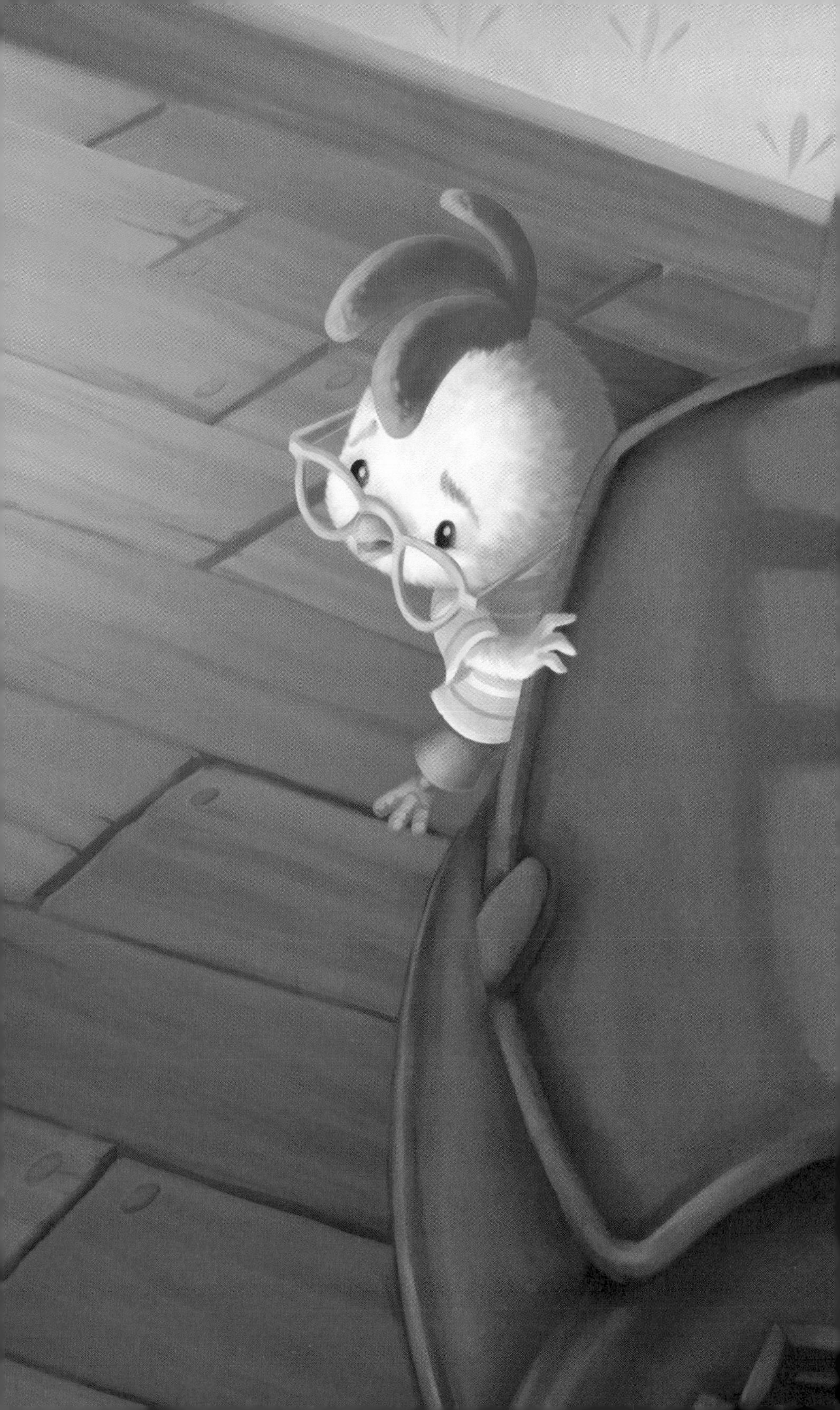

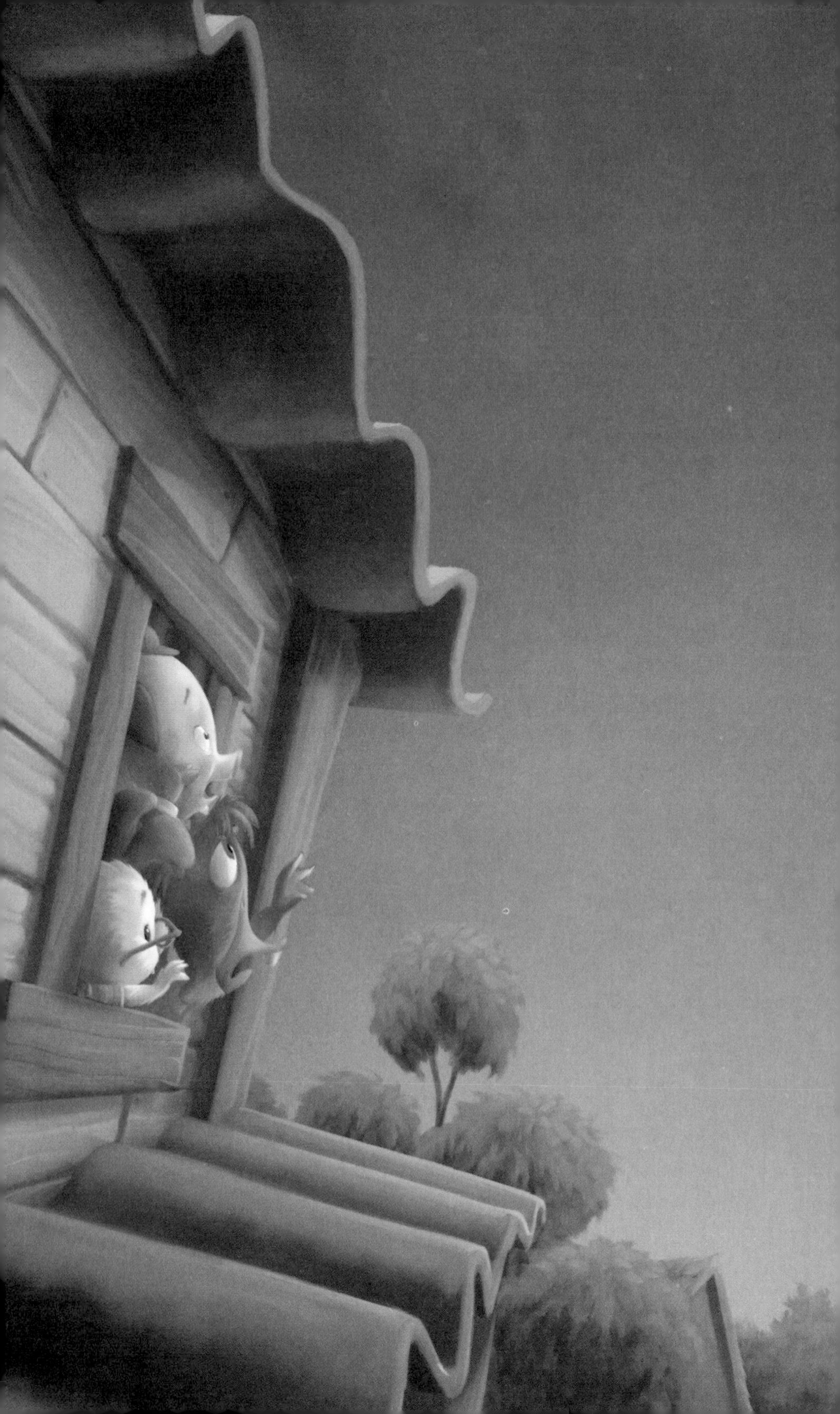

Fish, Abby, and Runt
came to help him.
Fish picked up
the piece of sky.
It floated in the air.
It flew out the window.
Fish flew out with it!

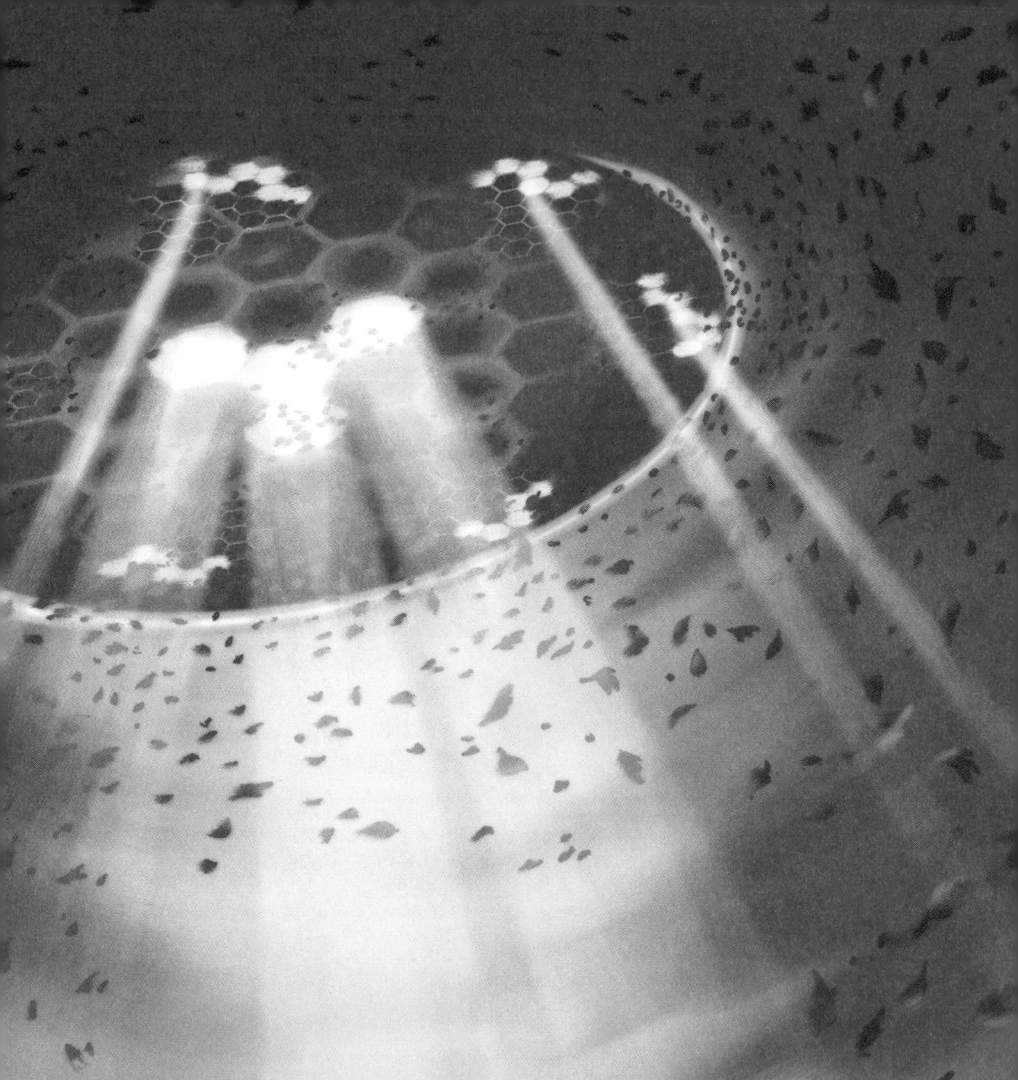

The friends raced
to help Fish.
They saw a spaceship
in the sky.

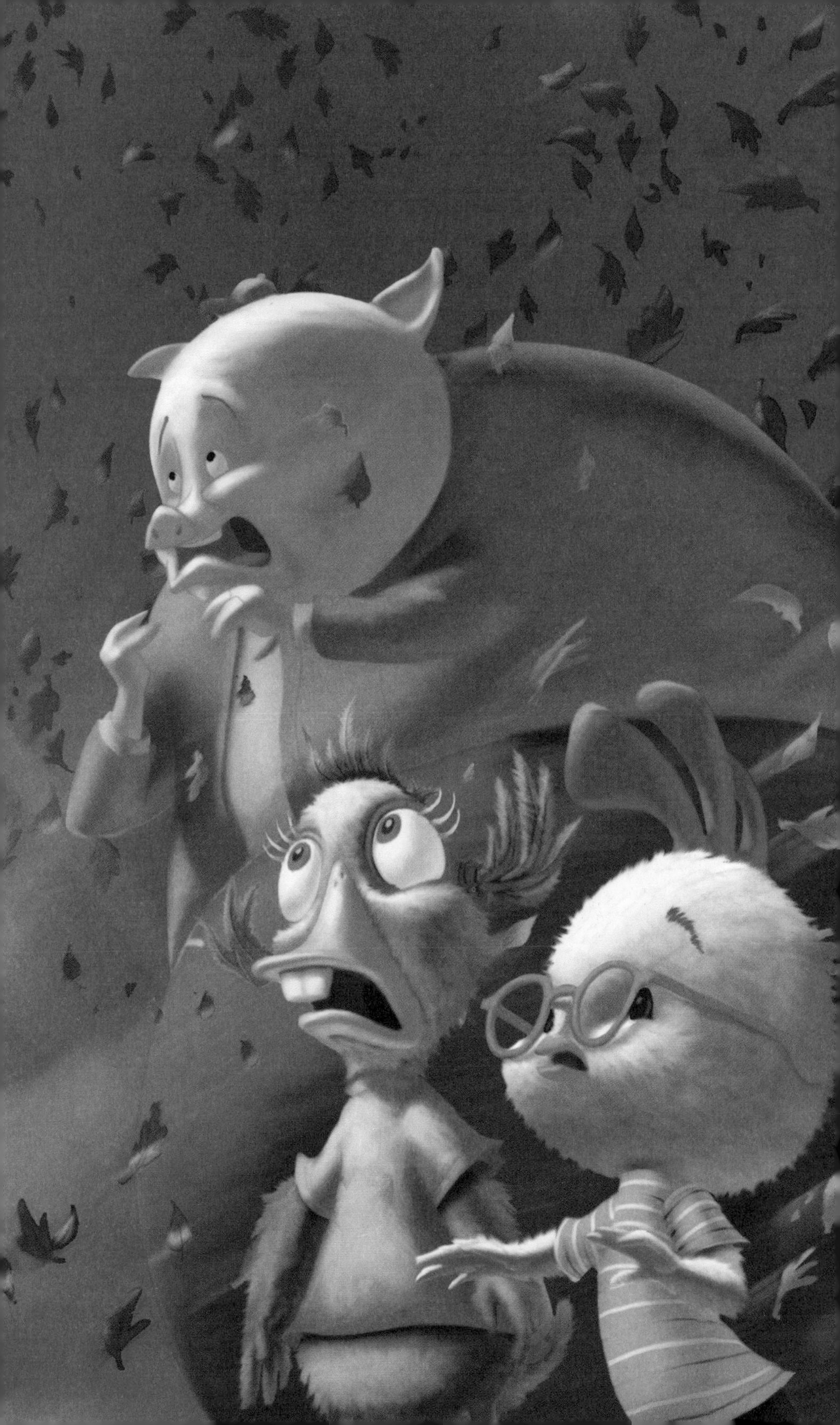

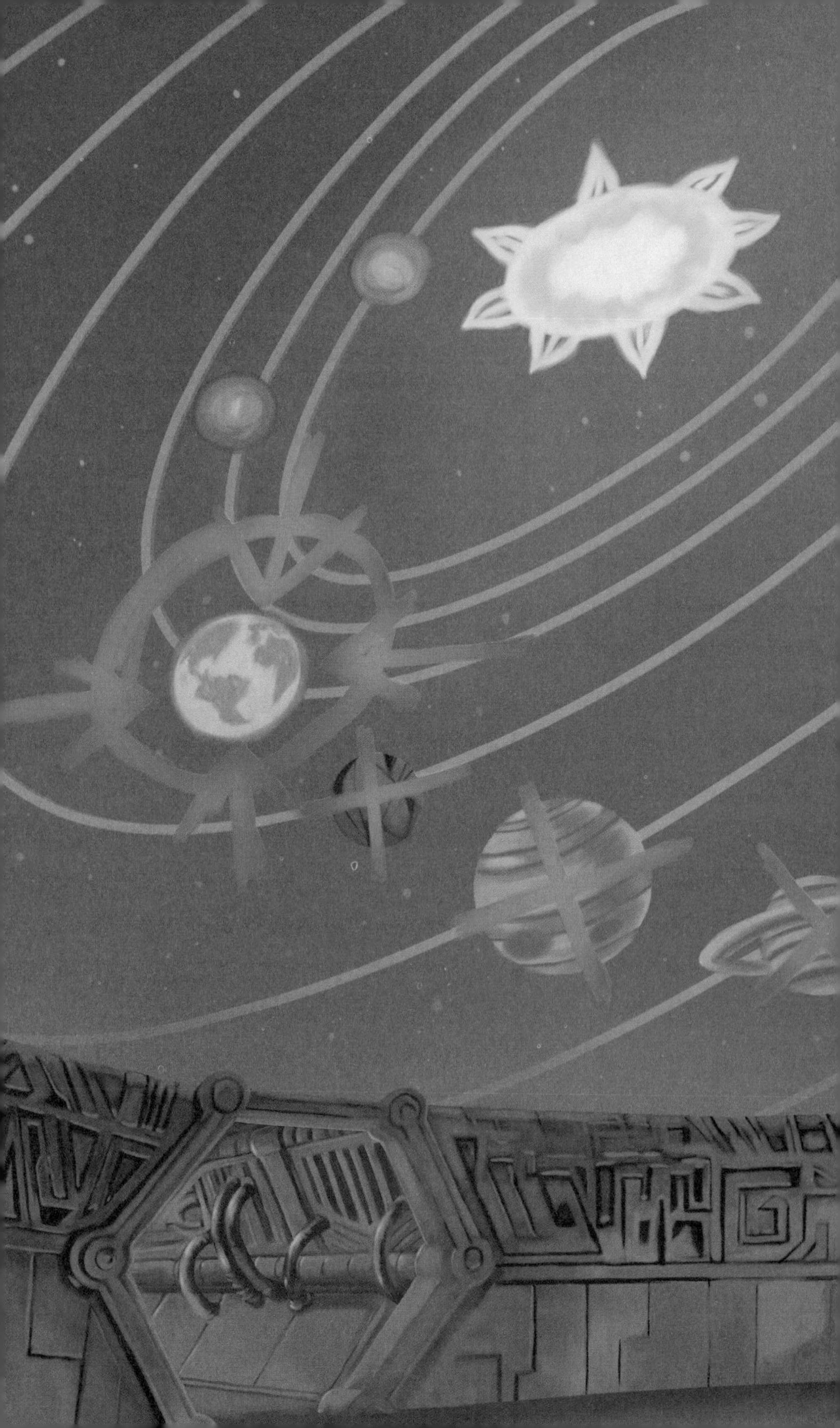

The friends snuck
onto the spaceship.
Fish was there!
And they learned that
Earth was in danger.
They had to tell
someone!

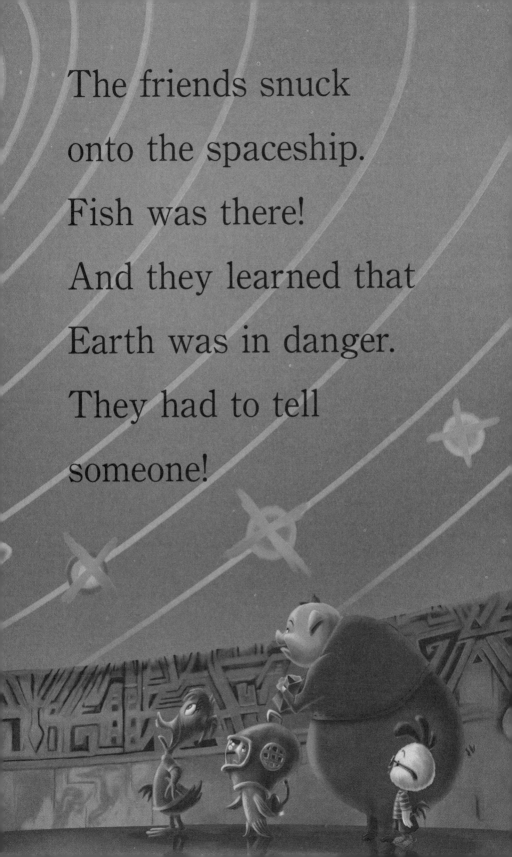

Chicken Little ran

to the school.

He rang the bell.

Ding! Dong!

"Aliens!" he cried.

"Aliens are here!"

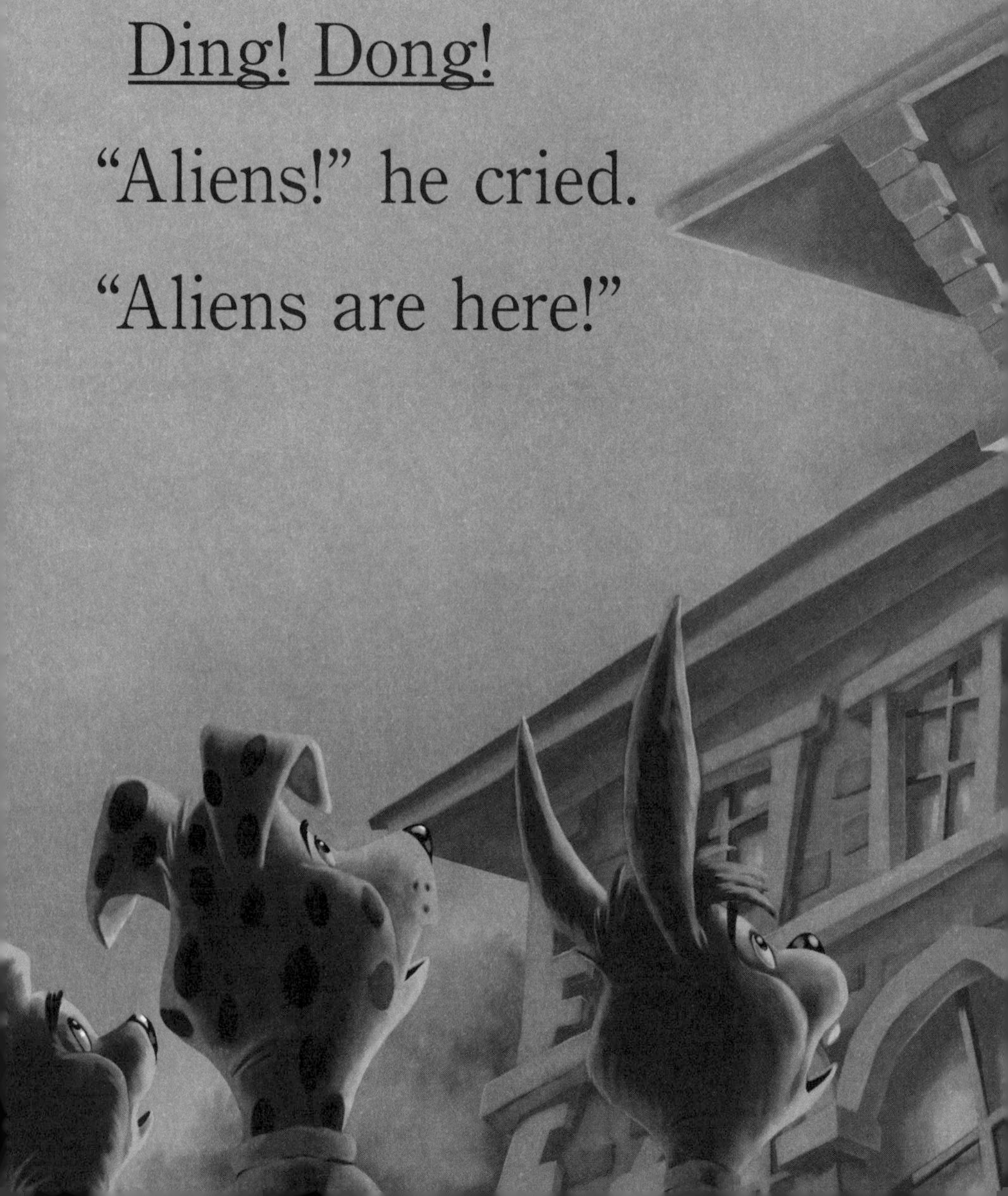

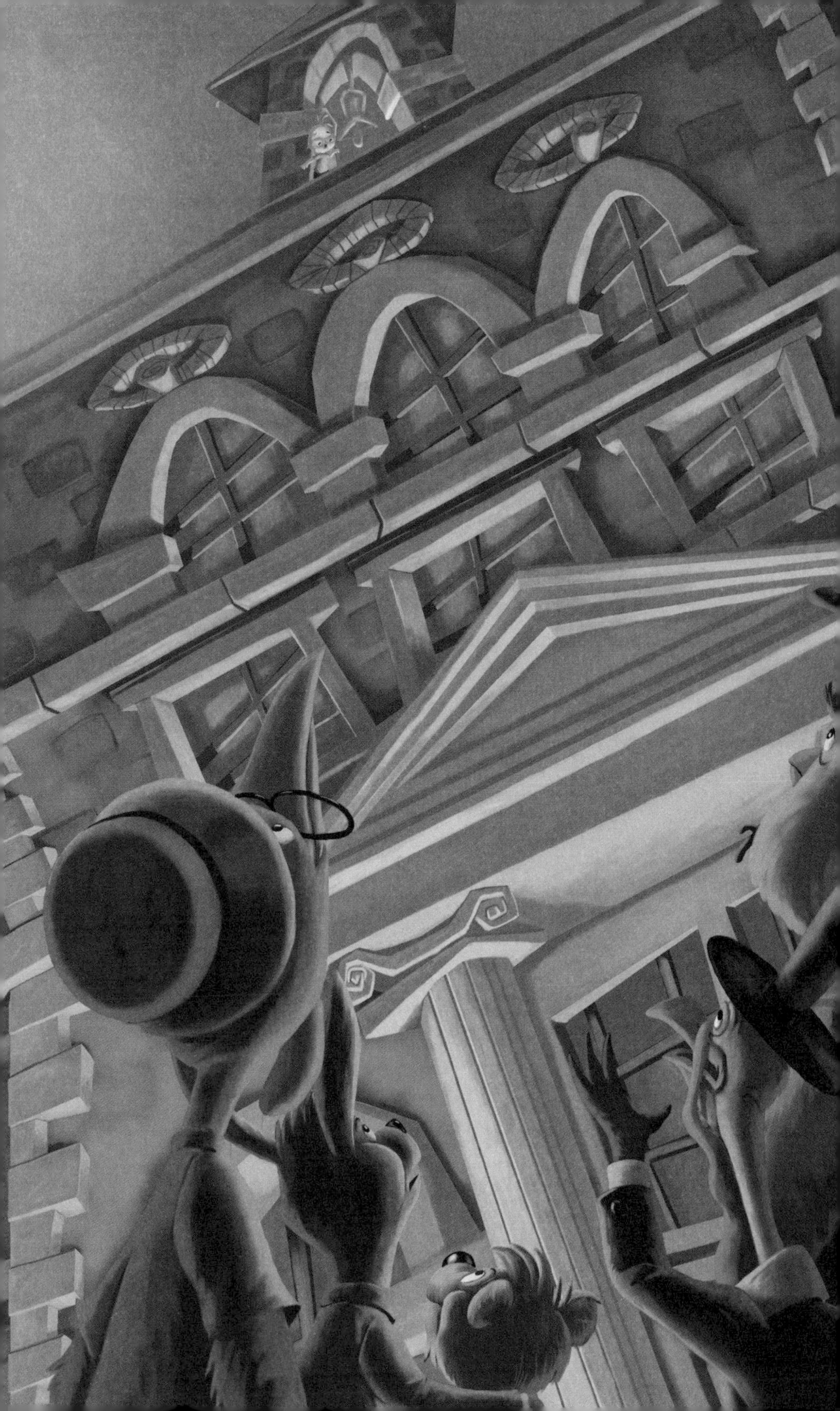

Everyone thought
Chicken Little
was crazy.
Even his dad.

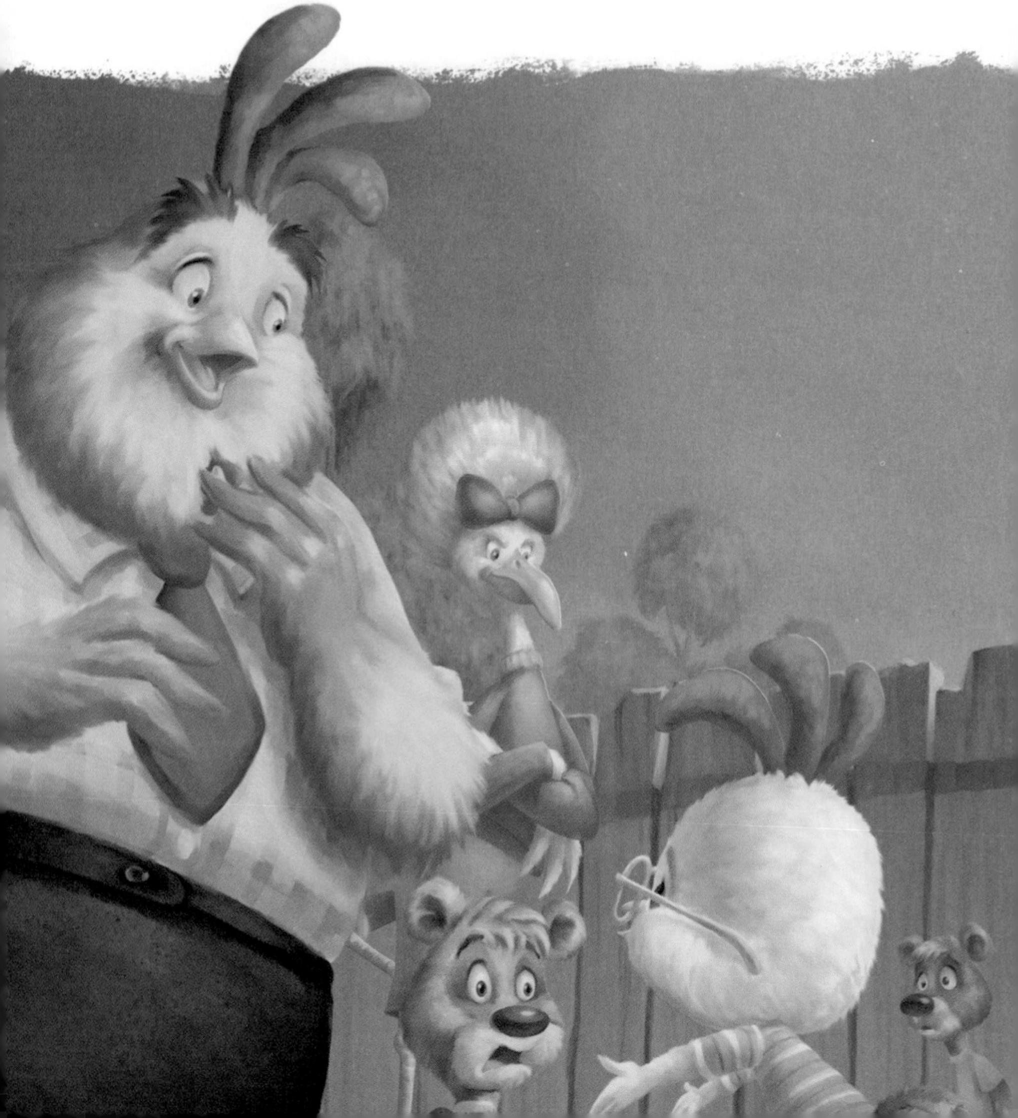

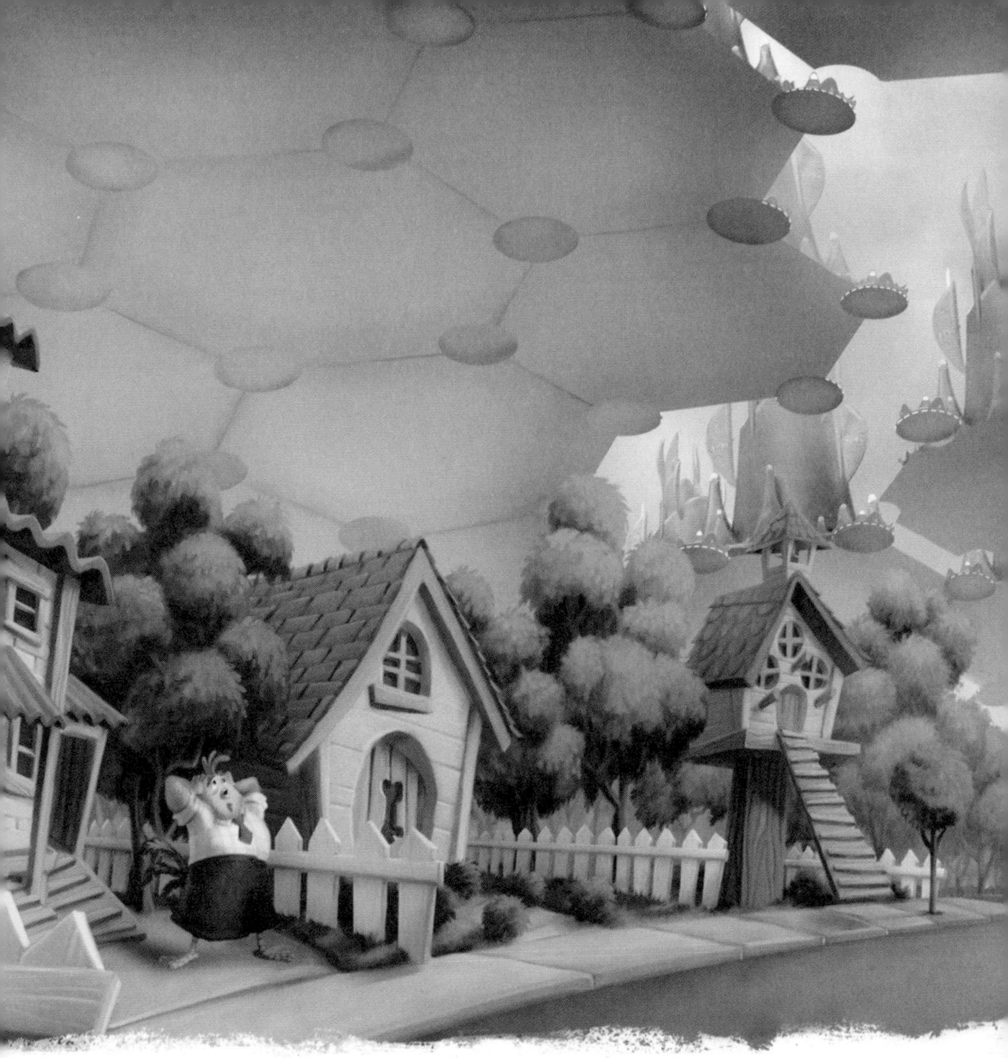

But soon Buck
saw it for himself.
The sky was
falling apart!

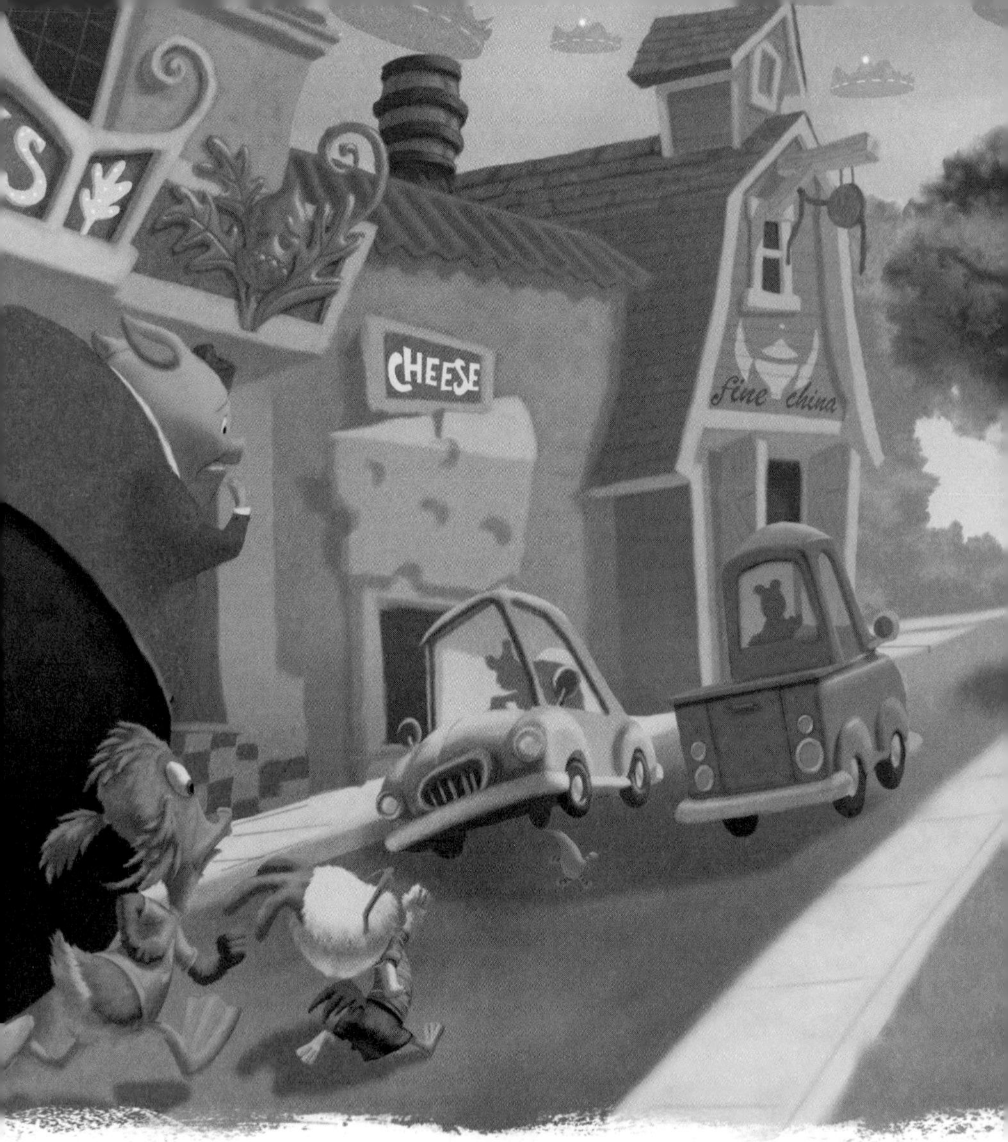
CHEESE
fine china

Chicken Little saw
an alien kid running.
He knew he was lost.

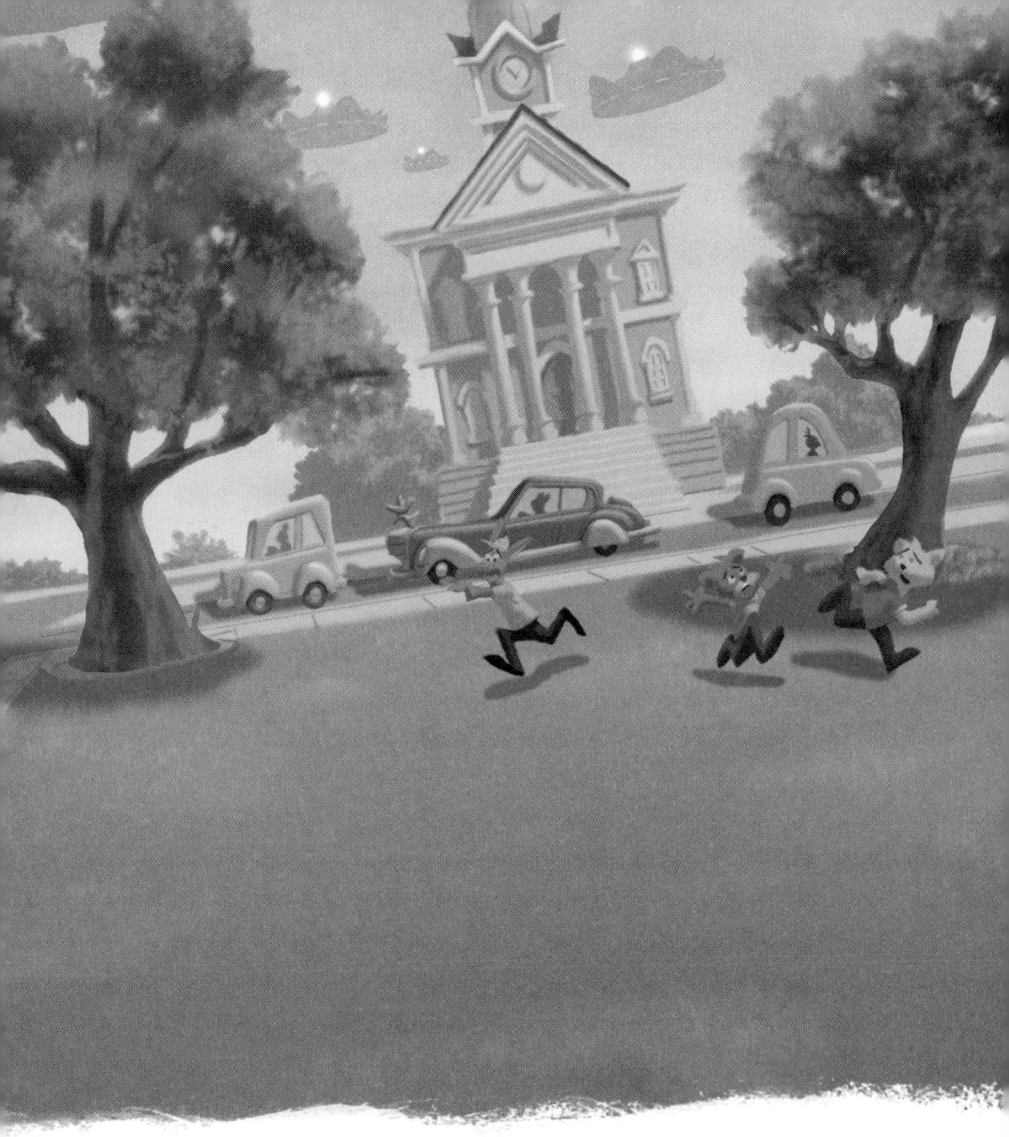

He had to return
the alien kid
to his parents.

Buck and Chicken Little faced the aliens.

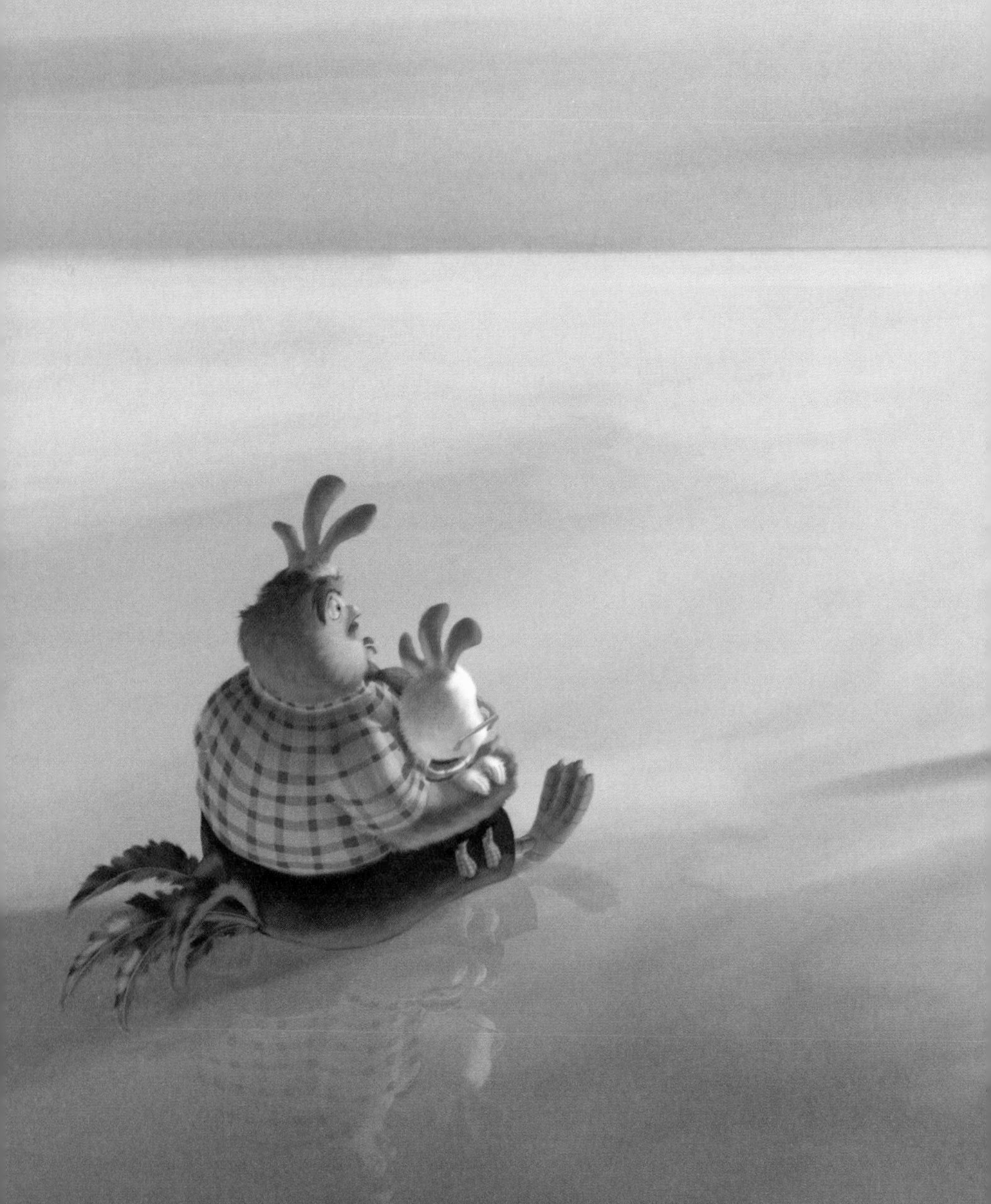

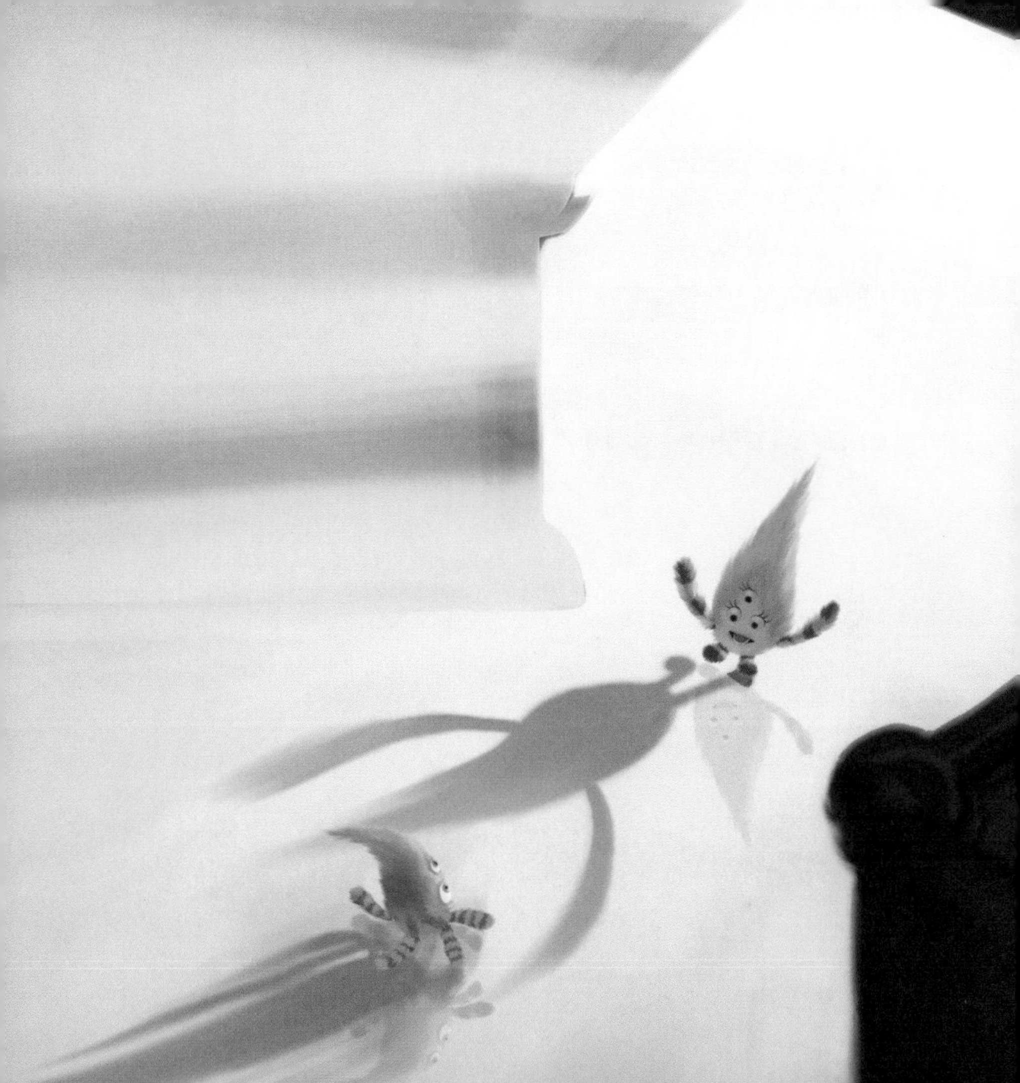

The Earth was not
in danger after all.
The aliens were only
looking for their child.

Chicken Little
gave the alien kid
back to his family.

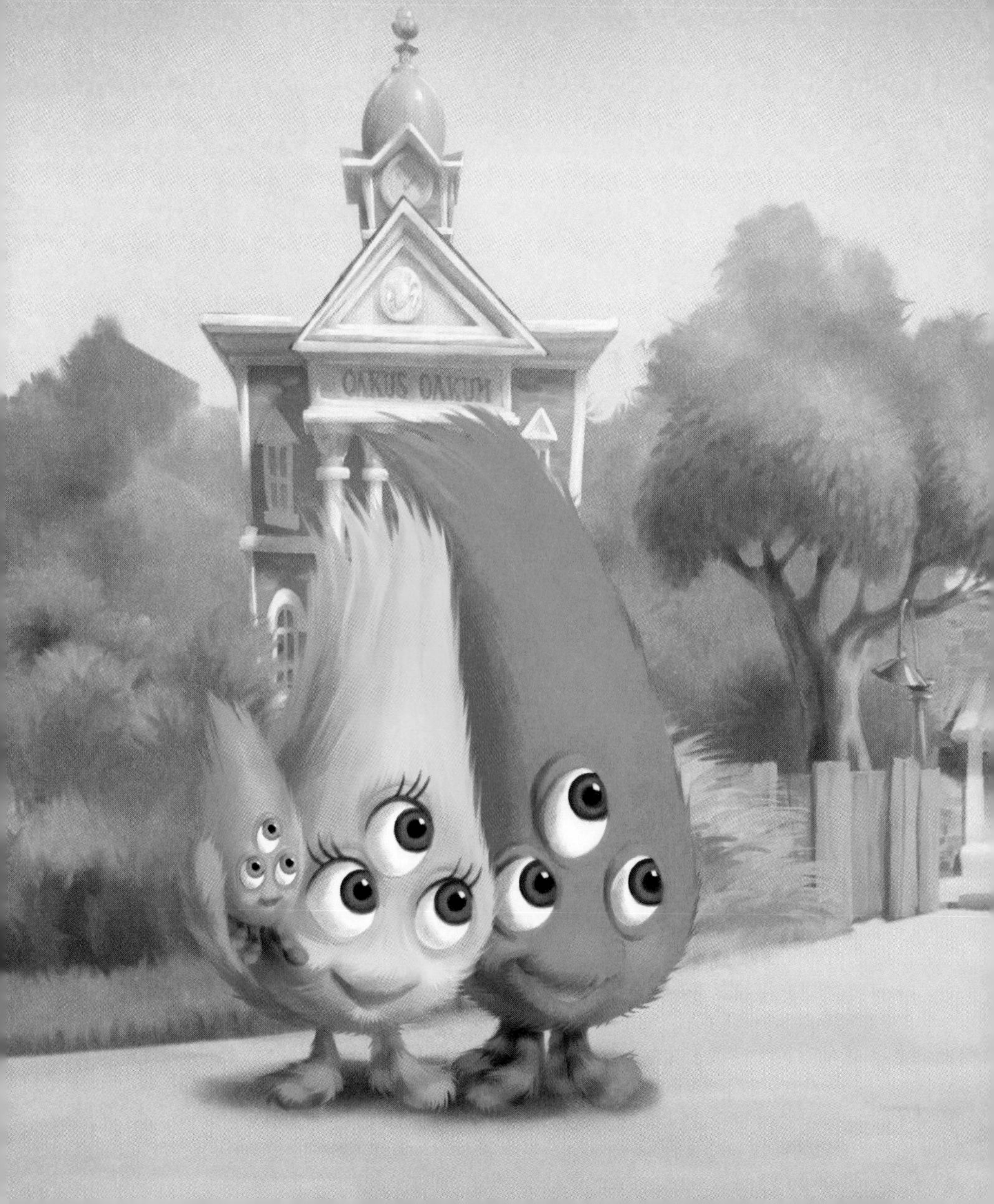

Now the aliens
could go home.
Chicken Little
was a hero!

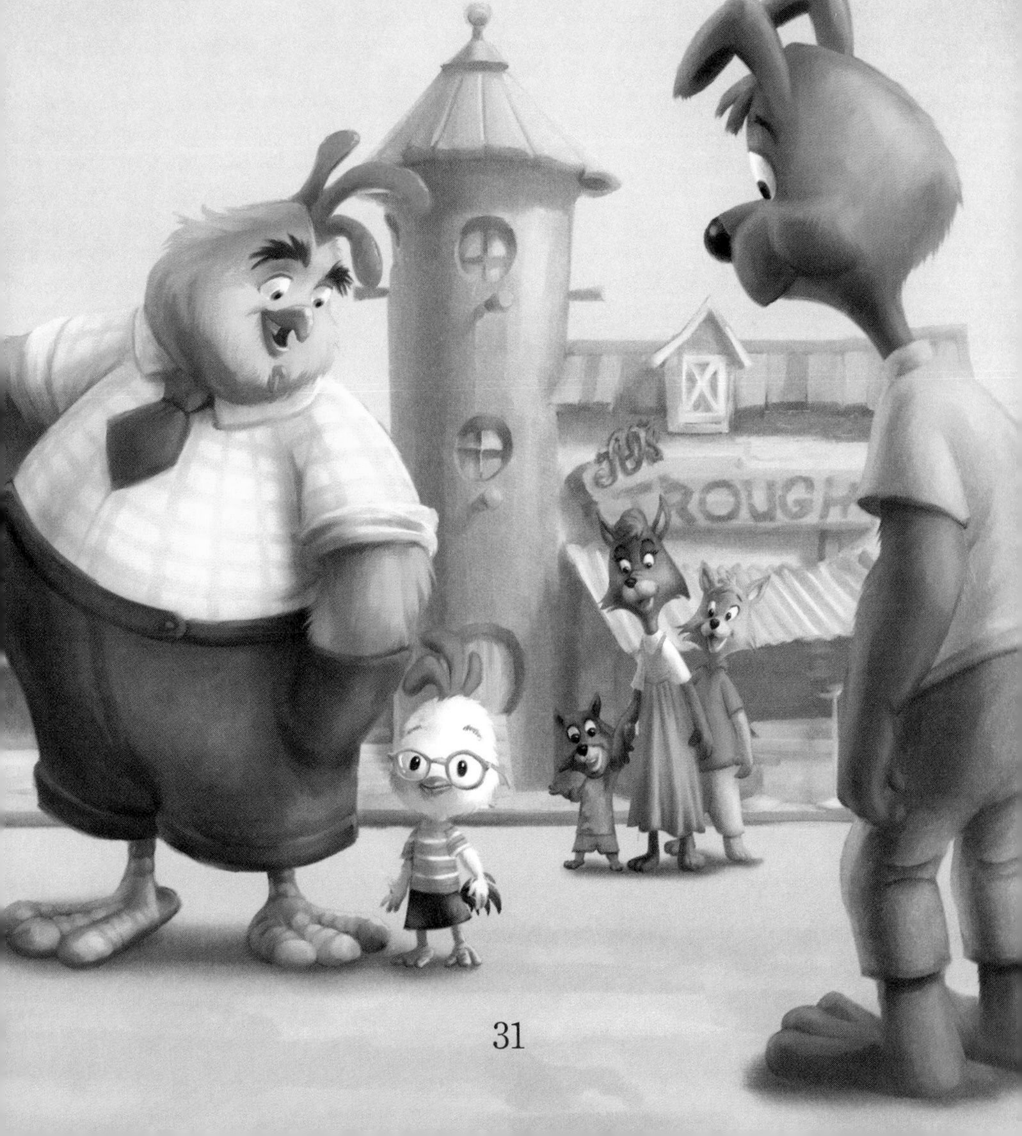

Things had changed after all!

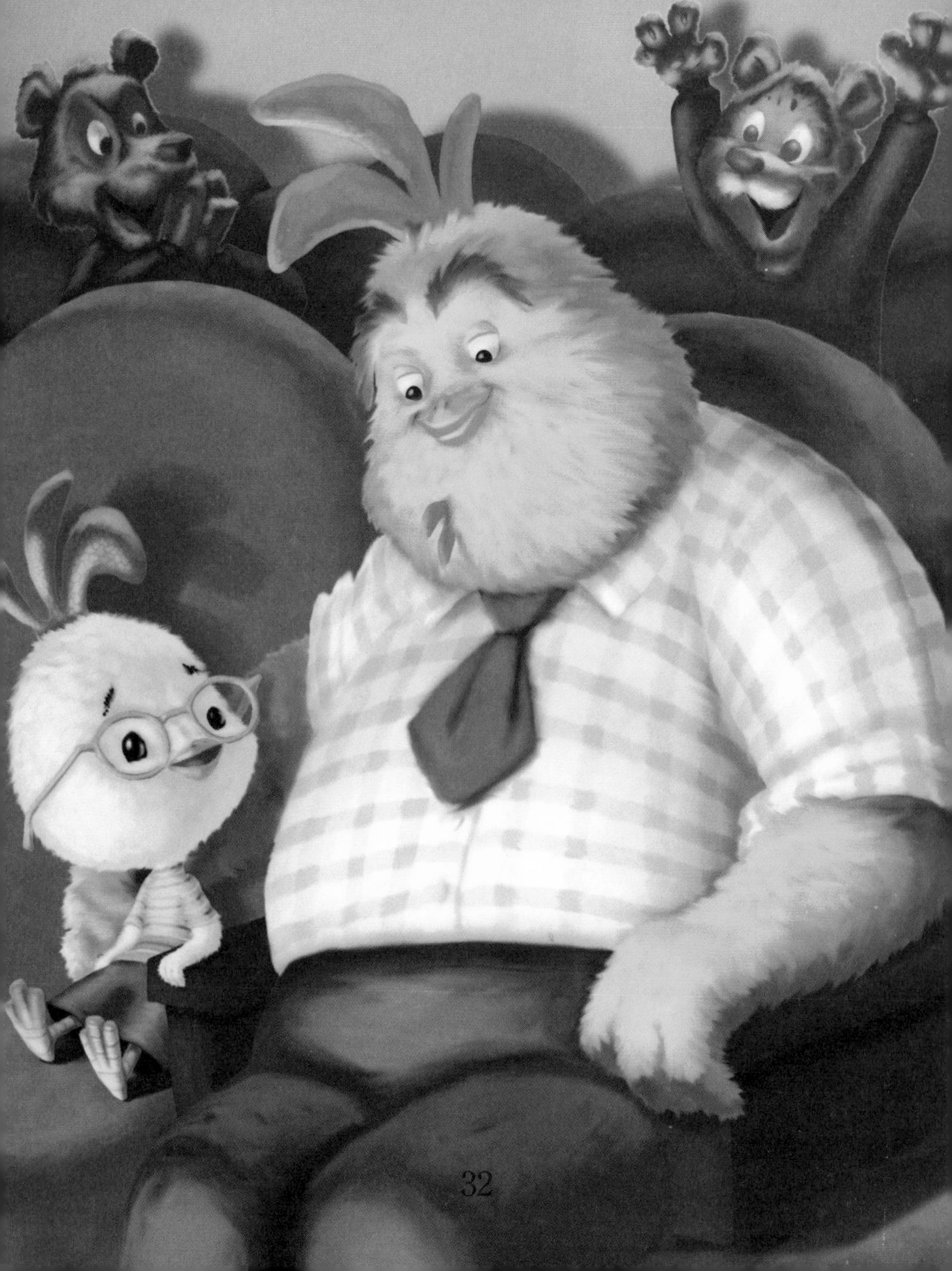

DATE DUE